This book is especially for
Rye, Bud, Karen, Gay and Alden Vervaet
who held in their mind the memory of the land
as it was and have returned it to us
to be loved by all.
Special thanks to Mag-la-Que,
Mahte-Topah, and Miyaca

Published by Dial Books
A Division of Penguin Books USA Inc.
375 Hudson Street
New York, New York 10014

5 7 9 10 8 6

Library of Congress Cataloging in Publication Data
Seattle, Chief, 1790–1866.
Brother eagle, sister sky : the words of Chief Seattle / paintings by Susan Jeffers.
Summary: A Suquamish Indian chief describes his people's respect
and love for the earth, and concern for its destruction.
ISBN 0-8037-0969-2.—ISBN 0-8037-0963-3 (lib. bdg.)
1. Indians of North America—Land tenure—Juvenile literature.
2. Suquamish Indians—Land tenure—Juvenile literature.
3. Human ecology—Juvenile literature.
[1. Indians of North America—Land tenure.
2. Suquamish Indians—Land tenure. 3. Human ecology.
4. Ecology. 5. Environmental protection.] I. Jeffers, Susan, ill. II. Title.
E98.L3S39 1991 811′.3—dc20 90-27713 CIP AC

The full-color artwork was prepared using a fine-line pen with ink and dyes.
They were applied over a detailed pencil drawing that was then erased.
The jacket art was based on a photograph
by Edward Curtis.

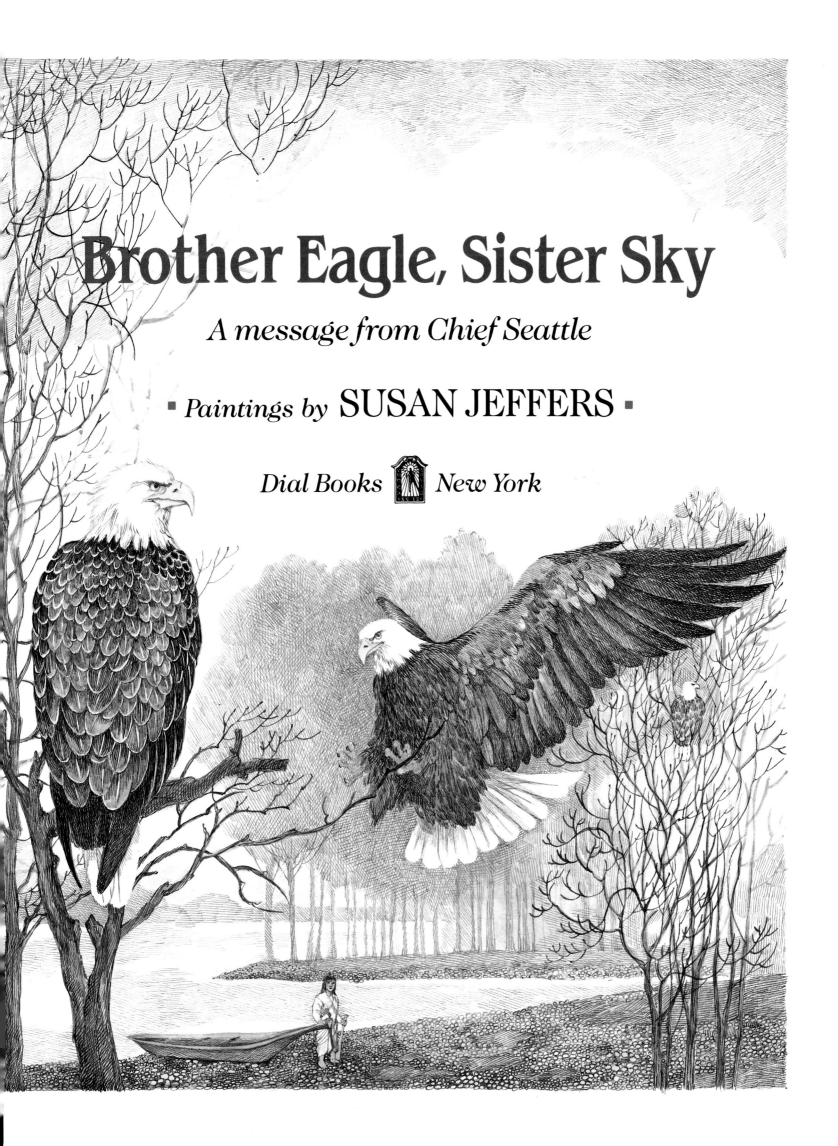

Brother Eagle, Sister Sky

A message from Chief Seattle

■ *Paintings by* SUSAN JEFFERS ■

Dial Books New York

In a time so long ago that nearly all traces of it are lost in the prairie dust, an ancient people were a part of the land that we love and call America. Living here for thousands of years, their children became the great Indian civilizations of the Choctaw and Cherokee, Navaho, Iroquois and Sioux, among many others. Then white settlers from Europe began a bloody war against the Indians, and in the span of a single lifetime claimed all the Indians' land for themselves, allowing them only small tracts of land to live on.

When the last of the Indian wars were drawing to a close, one of the bravest and most respected chiefs of the Northwest Nations, Chief Seattle, sat at a white man's table to sign a paper presented by the new Commissioner of Indian Affairs for the Territory. The government in Washington, D.C., wished to buy the lands of Chief Seattle's people.

With a commanding presence and eyes that mirrored the great soul that lived within, the Chief rose to speak to the gathering in a resounding voice.

How can you buy the sky? Chief Seattle began.
How can you own the rain and the wind?

My mother told me,
Every part of this earth is sacred to our people.
Every pine needle. Every sandy shore.
Every mist in the dark woods.
Every meadow and humming insect.
All are holy in the memory of our people.

My father said to me,
I know the sap that courses through the trees
as I know the blood that flows in my veins.
We are part of the earth and it is part of us.
The perfumed flowers are our sisters.

The bear, the deer, the great eagle, these are our brothers.

The rocky crests, the meadows,
the ponies—all belong to the same family.

The voice of my ancestors said to me,
The shining water that moves in the streams and rivers is
not simply water, but the blood of your grandfather's grandfather.
Each ghostly reflection in the clear waters of the lakes tells
of memories in the life of our people.
The water's murmur is the voice of your great-great-grandmother.
The rivers are our brothers. They quench our thirst.
They carry our canoes and feed our children.
You must give to the rivers the kindness you would give
to any brother.

The voice of my grandfather said to me,
The air is precious. It shares its spirit with all
the life it supports. The wind that gave me my first
breath also received my last sigh.
You must keep the land and air apart and sacred,
as a place where one can go to taste the wind that
is sweetened by the meadow flowers.

When the last Red Man and Woman have vanished with their wilderness,
and their memory is only the shadow of a cloud moving across
the prairie, will the shores and forest still be here?
Will there be any of the spirit of my people left?
My ancestors said to me, This we know:
The earth does not belong to us. We belong to the earth.

The voice of my grandmother said to me,
Teach your children what you have been taught.
The earth is our mother.
What befalls the earth befalls all the sons and daughters
of the earth.

Hear my voice and the voice of my ancestors,
Chief Seattle said.
The destiny of your people is a mystery to us.
What will happen when the buffalo are all slaughtered?
The wild horses tamed?
What will happen when the secret corners of the forest are
heavy with the scent of many men?

When the view of the ripe hills is blotted by talking wires?
Where will the thicket be? Gone.
Where will the eagle be? Gone!
And what will happen when we say good-bye to the swift pony
and the hunt?
It will be the end of living, and the beginning of survival.

This we know: All things are connected like the blood that unites us.
We did not weave the web of life,
We are merely a strand in it.
Whatever we do to the web, we do to ourselves.